DreamWorks

D1383014

SIMON SPOTLIGHT
An imprint of Simon & Schuster Children's Publishing Division
1230 Avenue of the Americas, New York, New York 10020
For information about special discounts for bulk purchases, please contact Simon & Schuster Special Sales at 1-866-506-1949
or business@simonandschuster.com.
Manufactured in the United States of America 1212 LAK
First Edition 1 2 3 4 5 6 7 8 9 10
ISBN 978-1-4424-4109-5
ISBN 978-1-4424-6142-0 (eBook)

Meet the Croods—Grug; his wife, Ugga; their children, Thunk, Sandy, and Eep; and Grug's mother-in-law, Gran.

The Croods spend most of their days in their cave, hidden safely away from the harsh outside world. For fun, Grug tells stories and draws on the cave walls. Every night the entire family sleeps in a large pile to stay warm and comfy.

Big, brave, and strong, Grug is the leader of the Croods family. His job is to protect and provide for them. He constantly reminds everyone to "never not be afraid." After all, the outside world is filled with dangerous animals. Bear Owls are creatures with the strength of a bear and an owl's night vision. Liyotes have lizard-like faces and coyote-like speed. And Trip Gerbils look adorable but will gladly knock you down to steal your food.

The Croods only leave the cave for one reason—to find food. "I want to see some real caveman action out there," Grug tells his family at the start of the hunt. First the Croods run to their hunting grounds. After they steal a breakfast egg from a Ramu bird, they have to make sure no other creatures steal it from them! It's a family effort, as the Croods toss, dribble, and run home with their breakfast egg.

One night Eep sneaks out of the cave. A mysterious light leads her to a strange animal. Eep grabs the creature and throws it to the ground.

The creature suddenly pulls off a mask. It's a boy!

"Ow!" the boy yells.

Eep is surprised.

"You talk!" she says.

"I'm a person, like you," he answers.

Eep is so strong that she lifts him off the ground with one hand.

"Sort of . . . like you," the boy says.

Guy introduces himself and his "pet," Belt. Guy can make the sun appear whenever he wants. He calls it "fire." Eep grabs Guy, shakes him, and tells him to make some fire for her.

"It doesn't come *out* of me!" Guy says.

When Eep tells her family that she left the cave and met someone new, named Guy, Grug is furious.

"New is a big problem," he tells Eep. "New is always bad!"

Suddenly the ground begins to shake. There is a massive earthquake. The family huddles in a tight ball under Grug.

When the earthquake is over, Croods Cave is completely gone. As they stand there wondering what to do next, a Bear Owl chases them off a cliff. The Croods have no choice but to venture into a vibrant new world.

Grug leads his family through the Jungle where they are quickly surrounded by Punch Monkeys. "I'll take care of this," Grug says and then launches into his threat display. "WAAAGGGhhhh!" he yells.

The Punch Monkeys laugh and take turns punching Grug in the face. They think this is lots of fun!

"Go get 'em, Dad!" Thunk cheers. But as the Punch Monkeys continue to beat up Grug, Thunk makes a suggestion. "Dad, I got it—just stop running into their fists."

Later the family thinks they've found a new cave! As soon as they are inside, the entrance slams shut.

"Hey, this cave has a tongue," Thunk says. "Awesome!"

The Croods had run straight into the mouth of a Land Whale.

Luckily for the Croods, the whale doesn't think they taste very good and shoots them right out through its blowhole.

And that's a good thing because a swarm of Piranhakeets suddenly appears and gobbles the entire Land Whale in a matter of seconds. Eep decides it's time to call Guy to help them in this strange New World. She blows on a horn.

Guy hears it and starts running toward the sound. He strikes a spark with two stones as the Piranhakeets close in. He keeps feeding the spark until it flares up into flames. Guy's plan works! The swarm of Piranhakeets is scared away.

Everyone is fascinated by Guy's fire. The Croods grab the embers. One of them falls on Thunk's tunic.

"It likes me!" he says. But then his clothing goes up in flames. "Hey! It's *biting* me! Ow! Stop!" he shouts.

Gran realizes her walking stick is on fire. She slams the stick down to put out the fire, but that starts more, smaller fires.

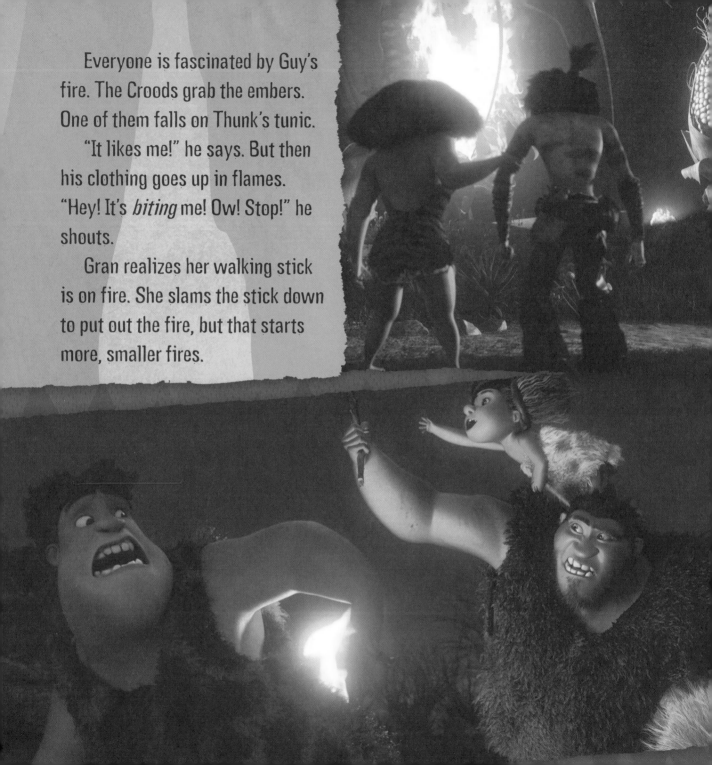

Gran pounds her stick with all her might, and the fire finally goes out—but not before lighting a cornfield on fire. Ears of corn soar into the sky and explode into popcorn like colorful fireworks.

Grug doesn't trust Guy.

"Your dad wants to kill me," Guy tells Eep.

"Yeah, but I won't let him," Eep answers.

Grug orders Guy to stay with the family until they find a new home. Guy suggests they head toward a high mountain, but Grug disagrees until he realizes caves will be there. The Croods will finally find a new home!

Grug tries to convince everyone the trip will be fun. "We'll tell stories. We'll laugh. We'll become closer as a family."

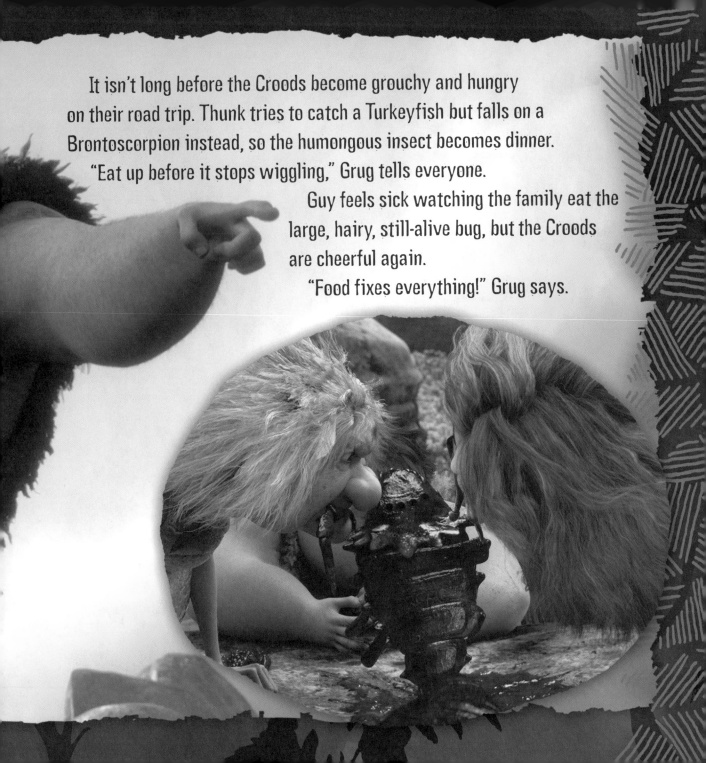

It isn't long before the Croods become grouchy and hungry on their road trip. Thunk tries to catch a Turkeyfish but falls on a Brontoscorpion instead, so the humongous insect becomes dinner.

"Eat up before it stops wiggling," Grug tells everyone.

Guy feels sick watching the family eat the large, hairy, still-alive bug, but the Croods are cheerful again.

"Food fixes everything!" Grug says.

Guy tells Eep he's hungry too.

"You can have some bug for dinner," Eep tells him. "There's plenty of bug!"

Instead Guy shows Eep how to set up a trap for the Turkeyfish.

After they catch the bird, they roast it over a fire. The Croods have never tasted anything so delicious, or anything cooked. "It's an avalanche of flavor," cries Thunk.

"Looks like we won't have any leftovers," Guy says as he watches the Croods chow down.

Eep asks him what a leftover is. "It's when you have so much food to eat you have some . . . left over," Guy explains.

"That never happens to us!" Eep declares.

As their journey continues, the Croods discover a coral field. They try to
walk across, but the sharp coral hurts their bare feet. Guy is wearing boots,
so he has no problem.

"Do not step on those weird, pointy rocks!" Grug warns.

Thunk shouts out suggestions to everyone. "Jumping on the rocks does not help.
Do not walk on your hands—the hands do not help at all!"

Guy thinks about leaving the Croods and heading for the Mountain on his own.

But he feels bad for the family and decides to help them. He makes everyone shoes out of leaves and fish.

Thunk looks down at his fishy feet. His shoes blink their eyes at him! "Aaaah!" he screams.

Eep and her mom admire each other's shoes.

"Ooh, I love those!" Ugga says about Eep's new shoes.

As the Croods get closer to the Mountain, they are blocked by a maze with many different entrances. Guy suggests they split up and each take a different route. But Grug is horrified. "Croods stick together," he says.

Suddenly the ground shakes again, and the Croods fall into different paths of the Maze. But instead of being scared, they have fun! Thunk plays catch with a Crocopup, while Eep discovers a flower that Guy left for her on her path. Gran and Ugga camouflage themselves in flowers to fool carnivorous plants.

Grug is the only one not having fun; he can't find his way out of the Maze. Reluctantly he blows on a shell and calls for help.

Once they reach the Mountain, a huge rift opens up in the ground, and the beautiful landscape before them vanishes. Nobody knows what to do, not even Guy.

Much to everyone's surprise, it is Grug who says the family must be separated. The only way to escape from the earthquakes is to get his family across the huge Chasm, so Grug explains that he will throw each of them across. Guy volunteers to go first.

"You know I've wanted to throw *you* away ever since I met you," Grug tells him.

Finally safe on the other side, the Croods are happy to be alive . . . but who will toss Grug to safety?

Grug doesn't need anyone to throw him—he decides to try something new. He puts together a flying invention.

"*Never* be afraid," Grug reminds himself.

His great idea gets him safely across the Chasm to his family. The Croods are back together and ready to explore a beautiful new world!